U0069419

故事崇拜

周士軒
Sean Chou

story
worship

目錄

Contents

故事崇拜

　　有些人的生命中不需要故事，因為他們的生活已經充滿了挑戰與刺激。或者他們的日常簡單而樸實乃至他們的心靈從來沒有收到過震撼，他們的視野從來不曾擴展。

　　但也有些（不）幸運的人們無法滿足於現實，或許他們已經達成了此生在世可能達成的一切目標，又或者他們一無所有，不曾有過任何成就，他們的生命空虛而無望，而且無力改變。

　　無論如何，這樣的人們需要故事，幻想，腦力的激盪，甚至癲狂的虛妄。不管是閱讀，撰寫，觀賞，描繪，創造或者遊玩，他們的人生需要故事來點綴。

　　我顯然是屬於需要故事的那類人。我需要故事，我渴望故事，因為如今的世界是如此的無趣煩人。或許有人會說我是在逃避現實，而我則回答：對啊，所以咧？不服你咬我啊？

　　遠離俗世的人被稱作隱士。

　　而用宗教當避世理由的則叫和尚，僧侶或修士

　　人們似乎敬重這些逃避現實的人們，有些甚至將他們敬如神明。但他們的信仰不比虛構的故事更現實到哪裡去。

　　甚至宗教的經典往往充滿了矛盾與過時封建的糟粕。

　　那將此身投更有趣，更感人，更有理的故事裡有什麼不對？

　　這就是我，隱於故事中的隱者，修行虛構的僧侶，察拜情感的祭司，傳道想像的牧師

　　創造的火花比那些騙子與神棍崇拜創造出的古老暴君更值得崇拜

　　故事是我存在的支柱，但我不會妄自菲薄的自稱自己是個偉大的作者。但故事不必複雜，因為根本上故事的存在價值是傳達知識與感情，只要您能將故事的主題傳達到的話它可甚至可以簡短到一句話，一抹色，一塊型。

　　話又說回來我究竟要講什麼樣的故事呢？那得依時時刻刻的心情，思考甚至健康狀況而定。當我心情好的時候我作品的筆觸與主題自然就更活潑，當我感覺差的時候我也不會迴避將之傾洩於畫布或其他的媒材上。或許有人會說我沒有一個連貫的風格或主題，但所謂風格無非是重複過往的成功，而我自認還沒有真正的達到能讓我滿意的境界。

　　總而言之，我是個愛故事的人，並邀請您一起參與到我的故事中。

Story Worship

I think it is fair to say that there are those who can live without stories, as their own day to day experience are more than enough to stimulate their mind. Or perhaps they live such a simple, humble existence that nothing had ever challenged their minds and expanded their horizons.

There are also those (un)fortunate souls who can't be satisfied by reality, whether it's because they already have everything that a man could possibly hope to achieve in this world and has grown tired of them

Or perhaps they had nothing, achieved nothing, living a hollow life with no real hope of changing their predicaments.

In any case, such men need fictions, fantasies, food for thought, nutrients of the mind, delusions of the mad. Whether it's to read them, write them, watch them, paint them, create them or play them. They need stories in their lives.

I certainly belong to the latter camp. I need stories, I crave stories, as the world today is so uninspiring and tiresome. Some would call this escapism to which I reply, yeah. It is. So? Gotta problem with that?

Those who escape from the world were called hermits.

Those who use religion as a excuse were called monks, priests and clergy

And for some reason people seems to ascribe certain moral or spiritual reverence to these escapees, even though their excuses were no more "real" than any fiction.

In fact most of their "excuse" were poorly written, filled with internal logical contradictions and bad moral lessons to follow

So what's wrong with devoting oneself to better written, better plotted, better meaning stories?

This is who, what I am. A hermit of stories, a monk of fictions, a priest of emotions and a clergy of imagination.

The spark of creativity and ingenuity is a much more worthy god to worship than any ancient despot conjured up by charlatans and madmen.

Story is the pillar of my very existence, though I would never dare claim myself to be a great storyteller. But stories don't have to be complicated, as fundamentally the point of a story is to convey ideas, emotions, and feelings, and if you get the message across, the story can be as simple as a sentence, a color, or even a shape.

Then what's the story that I want to tell? Well that really depends on the mood or thoughts, even physical wellbeing of mine at the moment of creating art. When I am in a good mood I tend to be more playful, both in terms of use of theme and techniques. When I feel awful I also do not shy away from spilling that all over the canvas, or any other medium that I happen to work on. Some would probably call this a lack of consistency or style, then again style is pretty much a repetition of success, and I haven't got any of those yet. At least not one that I am satisfied with.

In conclusion, I am someone who loves stories, and I welcome you to partake in them.

蝶 Butterfly　　53×46 cm　　acrylic on canvas　　2015

蝶

自灰色誕生的蝴蝶拍動它的翅膀
無風，無雨
甚至不能飛翔
自然沒有颶風

它雙翅的色彩在陽光下閃耀
沒有鼓掌，沒有喝彩
無人問津
如果註定無法在空中飛翔
蝴蝶是為何破繭而出？

Butterfly

The Butterfly born from gray flapped its wings
No wind, no rain,
Not even flight
Certainly no hurricane

Its bright colors shined beneath the sunlight
No applause, no cheers,
As nobody was in sight
To what purpose does the butterfly break out of the cocoon
If it was destined not to touch the sky?

深海的迷濛 Haze of Deep Ocean　46×53 cm　oil on canvas　2015

深海的迷濛

忘卻的夢想
忘卻的希望
記憶是個善變的情人
難以滿足，難以把持

Haze of Deep Ocean

Forgotten dreams
Forgotten hopes
Memory is a fickle mistress
Hard to please, hard to maintain

深海的夢想 Dream of Deep Ocean　　53×46 cm　　oil on canvas　　2015

深海的夢想

浮
睡
沉入夢鄉
遊
舞
溺入幻想
落至魂與靈的無底深淵
那無盡的黑暗是冷？是暖？

Dream of Deep Ocean

To Float

To Sleep

To Sink in Dreams

To Swim

To Dance

To drown in Fantasy

Down to the bottomless pit of soul and psyche

Is it cold down the deep dark abyss?

Or perhaps it's warm?

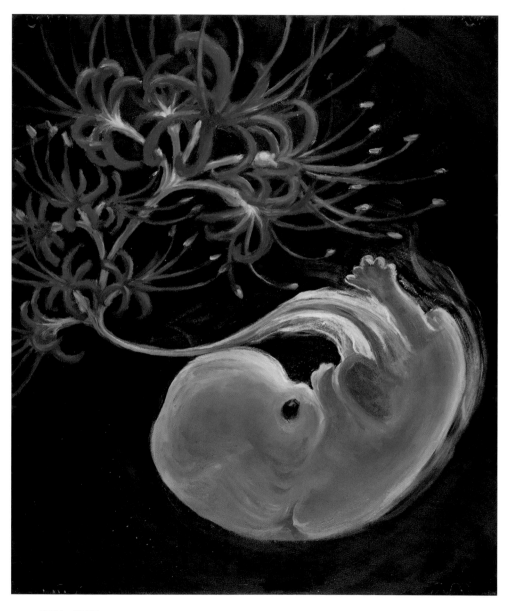

苦海 / 彼岸 Sea of woes/The shore beyond　　53×46 cm　　oil on canvas　　2017

苦海 / 彼岸

生於苦海

死往彼岸

沿路看到的風景值不值踏上艱辛的旅途？

已知結局的故事有沒有耗時聆聽的理由？

無念，無想，固然輕鬆

無趣，無聊，豈不可惜

難得走一遭

何不活個大汗淋漓？

何不死個頭破血流？

在苦海裡翻騰，也未嘗不痛快？

Sea of woes / The shore beyond

Born in the sea of woes

Die to the shore beyond

Would the scenery be worthy of the journey's hardship?

Is a story worth listening if you already know the ending?

Mindless, thoughtless,

that would be easy

Joyless, fun-less,

wouldn't that be a pity?

Why not get sweaty living?

Why not get bloody dying?

To twist and turn in the sea of woes, perhaps that in itself could be fun?

溶解 Dissolve　53×46 cm　oil on canvas　2015

溶解

失去知覺
失去自我
隨著邊界逐漸腐蝕，意識也隨之溶解
痛
苦
哀
絕望
創傷
挫敗
都如大海中的雨滴般消逝

Dissolve

Losing one's senses
Losing one's self
As the boundaries eroded, the mind dissolved
Pain
Suffering
Sadness
Despair
Trauma
Defeat
All gone, like a drop of rain in the Ocean

蒸汽夢想 Dream of Steam　46×53 cm　oil on canvas　2016

蒸汽夢想

過時

無用

多餘

可能有過的輝煌

或許能達到的繁榮

歷史的可能

過去時代的尖端早已腐朽

但浪漫猶在

夢想猶在

Dream of Steam

Out of fashion

Useless

Excessive

The glory that could have been

The prosperity that might have had

The possibilities of history

What was once the cutting edge had long corroded,

But the romance was still there

The dream was still there

傀儡之王 King of Puppets　　72.5×60 cm　　acrylic on canvas　　2015

傀儡之王

傀儡為扯線人所操作，但扯線之人何嘗不為傀儡而存在？

King of Puppets

A puppet has its puppeteer, but doesn't the puppeteer exist for the puppet?

面容 Faces　72.5×60 cm　acrylic on canvas　2015

面容

哈羅，我說道
你好，俺回答
日安，吾云之
我，俺，吾，鄙，余
我為眾然我獨在
人前的我
人後的我
鏡中的我
鏡頭前的我
與同輩談笑的我
與師長商討的我
咒罵蒼天的我
熱愛大地的我
有著千千萬萬的我，但我仍舊孤獨
有著千千萬萬張臉，但我仍舊孤獨
我獨在
不全，痛苦的獨在

Faces

Hello, says I.
Greetings, says me.
Salute, says moi.
I, I, I, I, I
I am many and yet I am one
To be alive is to have many "Is"
The I in front of you
The I in front of me
The I when I look myself in the mirror
And the I when I stare into the camera
The I who talk to my peers
The I who speak to my mentors
The I who curse the Heavens
And the I who loves the Earth
With so, so many "Is" around, one would think that I would not be alone
Yet not matter how many "Is" there are, how many faces I have
I am but one
A dysfunctional, tormented one

炎 Flame　72.5×60 cm　acrylic on canvas　2015

炎

燃燒，即是變化
從一種形態變成另一種
放出熱光與能量
變得暗淡
燃盡，焦黑，枯萎
死去
生命，即是變化
從一種形態變成另一種
在這世間留下印記
變得暗淡
衰老，疲憊，枯萎
死去
生命，即是燃燒

Flame

To burn, is to change,
From one form to another
Relcasing heat, light, energy
And become something dull,
Burnt, blackened, spent
Dead
To live, is to change
From one form to another
Making an impact and leaving one's mark
Then become something dull
Aged, tired, spent
Dead
To live, is to burn

扭曲 Twist　72.5×60 cm　acrylic on canvas　2016～2020

扭曲

變化的五彩
隨意的揮灑是神來之筆還是無用之功？
伸張的形體
奇妙的變化是畫外之音還是言之無物？
漆黑的背景
冗長的時空是精雕細還是磨苟延殘喘？
扭曲的畫面
一瞬的靈感是正中靶心還是無的放矢？

Twist

Changing colors
Were the random strokes an act of genius or one of naught?
Expanding forms
Were the morphing shapes a meaningful echo for a pointless rant?
Blackened background
Was the expanded time the soft fire making sweet malt or the languish of the sick?
Twisting sight
Were the momentary inspirations hitting the bullseye or missing the mark?

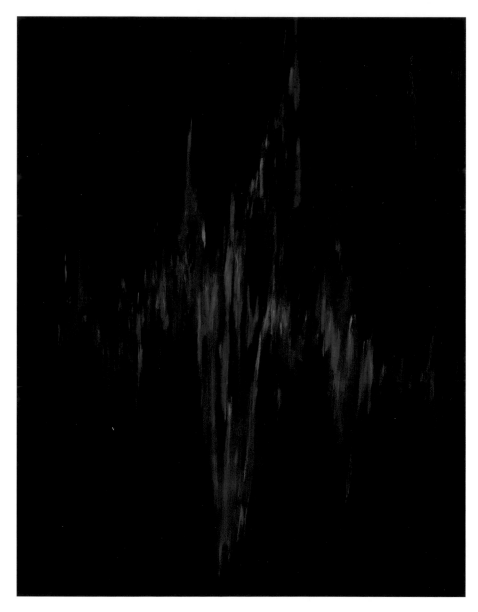

脈動 -1 Pulse-1　　117×91 cm　　oil on canvas　　2019

脈動 -1

血脈的鼓動
心臟的跳動
音樂的節奏
靈魂的律動

Pulse-1

The pulses of veins
The beats of hearts
The rhythm of music
The melody of soul

脈動 -2 Pulse-2　　117×91 cm　　oil on canvas　　2019

脈動 -2

無心的鼓動
無意的跳動
無想的節奏
無盡的律動

Pulse-2

Careless pulses
Mindless beats
Thoughtless rhythm
Endless melody

夢幻泡影 Dreams and Shadow　117×91 cm　oil on canvas　2019

夢幻泡影

一切有為法，
如夢幻泡影；
如露亦如電，
應作如是觀。
----《金剛般若波羅蜜經》偈頌

Dreams and Shadows

All things contrived are like
Dream, illusion, bubble, shadow,
And as dewdrop or lightning,
They should be regarded as such.
-----<The Diamond Sutra> Gatha

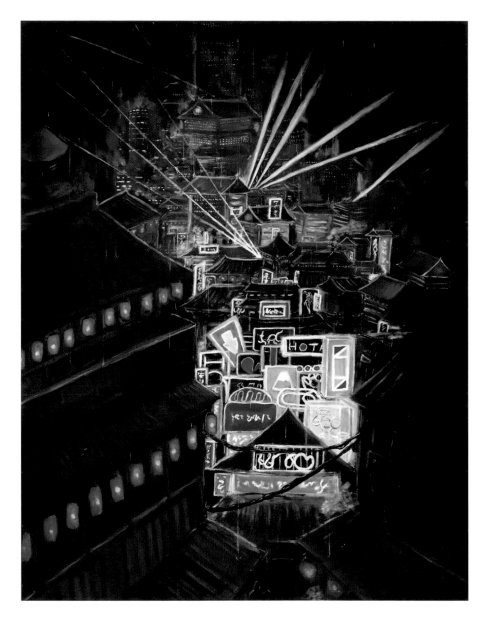

夜 Night　117×91 cm　oil on canvas　2017

夜

夜幕之下
霓虹的光彩攝人心魂
尋歡的人在巷間穿梭
迷人的色香引人入勝
叫賣夜晚暫靠的港灣
絢麗繁華的背後總是充滿了不堪
光鮮亮麗的陰面往往居住著黑暗
醉在絢麗的夜晚裡
生在溫柔的謊言中
夢在巧妙的演出裡
死在頹廢的迷茫中
夜，總是那麼誘人
夜，總是那麼可怖

Night

Under the veil of the night
The Neon lights mesmerized the heart
As revelers traversed the alleys
The luring scent pulled them closer
While they called ships to their night harbor
The shadow of prosperity was always filled with the despicable
The hidden face of glamour had always harbored darkness
To drown in the splendor of night
To live in the tenderness of lies
To dream in well-choreographed acts
To die in decadent wander
The night, is always so alluring
The night, is always so frightening

唐吉珂德 Don Quixote　117×91 cm　oil on canvas　2019

唐吉珂德

我思故我在
既然你無法證明我並非漂浮在容器中的腦髓
那我又何必為你放棄我所沉醉的夢想？
面對現實雖是必要
但向不公與無趣妥協又有何高貴？
不如做個與風車決鬥的騎士
不如沉浸在高尚的夢想中
心中常駐正義與俠情

Don Quixote

I think, therefore I am
Since you can't prove that I am not a brain
floating in a jar
Then why should I abandon my fantasies for your enjoyment?
Sure it's important to face reality
But what's so noble about compromising to injustice and boredom?
Might as well be the knight who duels the windmill
Might as well immerse in a noble dream
With justice and chivalry in heart

生 Growth　117×91 cm　oil on canvas　2020

生

共生
寄生
變生
夏草不曾問過冬蟲的意見
蛔蟲哪會想到腸胃的痛楚
生食死物
生生息息
死誕新生
萬物流轉

Growth

Symbiosis
Parasitism
Metamorphosis
The fungus never asked the opinion of the caterpillar
The roundworm wouldn't care about the pain of the stomach
The living eats the dead
Such is how life propagate
The dead births new life
Such is how the cycles turn

旅途

旅人

孤獨的旅人走在路上　　一步，一步　　一步，又一步
穿過黑暗的叢林　　走進荒廢的古城　　看見酣睡的巨人　　仰望漫天的星辰
哪裡才能找到答案？
哪裡才能獲得救贖？

孤獨的旅人走在路上　　一步，一步　　一步，又一步
掉入無底的深淵　　遇見海底的女王　　參加夢幻的茶會　　眺望雲上的城邦
溫暖躲藏去了哪裡？
幸福又迷失在何方？

在那迷茫的夜晚　　他找不到方向　　走過千里的現在　　迷了路又何妨

孤獨的旅人走在路上　　一步，一步　　一步，又一步
走入絢爛的市集　　買齊冒險的行裝　　踏進無盡的沙漠　　仰望七彩的幻光

Journey

Traveler

The lone traveler walks the road   Step by step   One step and another step
Through the dark woods   Into the ruins
Seeing the sleeping giant   And gaze upon the stars
Where could he find the answers?
Where could he find his salvation?

The lone traveler walks the road   Step by step   One step and another step
Fall down the bottomless abyss   Meeting the Queen of the deep
Attending a fantastical tea party   And gaze upon the city above the clouds
To where did warmth hide?
To where did happiness was lost?

In that wandering night   He had lost his bearings
Having walked for a thousand miles   Might as well just stay lost

The lone traveler walks the road   Step by step   One step and another step
Walk into the dazzling market   Shop for the journey to come
Enter the endless desert   And gaze upon the riotous aura

旅途—異象 Journey - Anomaly　65×80 cm　oil on canvas　2016

異象

　　旅人走在大漠中。與無數在到達這點前早已放棄，然後在尋找出路的途中永遠迷失的先人不同，他一步步的向沙漠的深處走去。究竟已經過去幾小時，幾天，或者幾個月了？誰知道呢？在沙漠中的旅途已經讓旅人失去了時間的概念，漫天的沙暴讓他無法睜眼他甚至無法從周邊的環境來辨別究竟是白晝或是黑夜。

　　風暴終究過去了，但沙漠並沒有減緩絲毫的敵意。太陽幾乎令人憎恨的耀眼，不斷的燃燒者旅人的氣力。放眼所見一路延伸到地平線外的只有無盡的沙丘，每一步都陷入滾燙的沙中，而將腳從坑中拔起也越來越費力。旅人早已用盡了他所有的補給，唯一支持他的身體向前行的僅有一樣東西，管它叫意志，決心，信仰，瘋狂，或者任何可以形容他心中那扭曲深淵的字眼，無論如何旅人依舊一步步的向前邁進。

　　那一刻，他踏出了那與其他千萬步相同的步伐，但下個瞬間彷彿是跨過了至今阻擋了視線的帷幕，旅人眼前的景色驟然一變，他抬起頭，帶著敬畏看著眼前的景象，他立刻理解了在他眼前的便是他尋求已久的東西。在那短暫的一瞬他疑惑沙漠的炎熱是不是終究摧毀了他的理智讓他看到了幻象，但他知道即使是在最瘋狂的醉夢中他的大腦也沒能耐想像出此刻在他眼前的事物。

　　他開始奔跑，即使一切的常理都指出他不可能有還有奔跑的餘力。在從天際灑落下的不斷變化的彩光照耀下他逐漸接近他的目標。他嘗試大笑，但發出的只有喘息與咳嗽。他幾乎能感到全身的每一個細胞都在發出悲鳴，在 "它" 的座前逐漸分崩離析，因為常人根本不該來到 "它" 的跟前。但一切的苦痛都無法與他心中的狂喜相提並論。

　　於是，旅人的旅途結束了

　　於是，旅人的旅途正要開始

Anomaly

A lone traveler was walking into the Great dessert. But unlike many others who'd give up at this point and try to turn back, only to get lost in the raging storm forever, this traveler got deeper into the dessert, braving through the storm one step at a time. Hours, days, or perhaps months has passed. Who knows? The traveler had long lost track of time. Even if he wanted to tell by his surroundings, the veil of sandstorm had made visibility close to none.

Eventually though the sandstorm passed, but the dessert didn't become any less hostile. The sun above was shining brightly, almost despicably so, and kept burning away the traveler's strength. All he could see was an endless expanse of sand dunes continuing all the way to the horizon and beyond. With each step his feet sunk into the hot burning sand and took ever increasing effort to pull them out. The supplies he got ran out long ago, and there was only one thing fueling his body forward. Call it his will, determination, faith, obsession, madness, or however you wish to call the swirling abyss in his mind.

He took another step which seemed the same as all of the countless ones he has took before, but suddenly the view in front of him changed, as if he had stepped through an invisible veil which blocked the sight in front of him until this moment. He looked up towards the sky in awe, and knew immediately this is it, what he was looking for all along. The idea of this being nothing but a trick of light, or some sort of hallucination created by his over-heated mind quickly crossed his mind. But he knew that even in the wildest state of dream or intoxication, his mind was not capable to creating something like what's in front of him at this moment.

He began to run, despite all reason suggesting his body was in no condition of doing so. Illuminated by the colorful, ever-changing light coming from above, he came closer and closer to his goal. He felt like laughing, but what came out was more akin to desperate gasps and coughing. He could almost feel each and every cell in his body screaming, crumbling and dying in "its" presence, as no mortal should have come so close to such a "thing". But all the pain was nothing compared to the maddening joy filling his mind.

And thus, the traveler's journey has ended.

And thus, the traveler's journey has begun.

旅途—大圖書館 Journey - Great Library　80×65 cm　oil on canvas　2016

大圖書館

大圖書館入館須知

進入本館請配合以下事項。違規可能導致負傷，詛咒，死亡，乃至魂飛魄散。

1. 進入館藏區前請先至入口服務台進行登記。本館不保障未登記者的人身安全。
2. 不得攜帶武器，食物，飲料，寵物，使魔，哥雷姆等進館。
3. 禁止使用任何種類的元素魔法。如有需要使用身體強化或翻譯魔法請先在入口服務台登記。
4. 請保持肅靜，以防被對聲音敏感的生物襲擊
5. 請勿在館內獵殺其他的使用者。
6. 本館館藏的書籍很多都擁有自我意識，請務必友善對待它們。若使用者與書籍間發生任何衝突請自行解決。
7. 請勿擅自將書籍帶離原本所在的區塊以防觸動封印結界。
8. 若有需要在浮游平臺間移動請洽附近的圖書館員甲蟲。它們會很樂意為您服務。
9. 個人物品在離館時須悉數攜出，本館不負遺失賠償責任。

本館不為在館內因書籍造成的任何生理，心裡，靈魂上的傷害，死亡，消滅事件負責。

如有任何疑問，請洽入口訊問台。

Great Library

Terms and Condition of The Great Library

During your visit please adhere to the following regulations. Any violation may result in long term injury, curses, death, or eternal damnation.

1. Please register at the reception before entering the collection. This library does not guarantee the safety of un-registered visitors.
2. Do not carry any weapon, food, drink, pet, familiar or golem into the library.
3. All forms of elemental magic are forbidden. If you wish to use physical enhancement or translation magic please register at the reception.
4. Please remain quiet, to prevent being attacked by voice sensitive creatures.
5. Please do not hunt other visitors in the library.
6. Many of this library's collection are self-aware, please be kind to them. Any disagreement between the visitor and the collection in question should be dealt with on your own.
7. Please do not take the book outside of their original area, or it may trigger the entombment barrier.
8. If you need to move between the floating platforms please ask any of our librarian beetles. They are always glad to be your help
9. Please take all of your belongings with you when leaving. The library is not responsible for any loss or reparation.

The Great Library is not responsible for any physical, psychological, or spiritual injury, death, annihilation resulting from interaction with the collection.

隨筆-1

病
昏昏沉沉
迷迷茫茫
病痛中的夢境總是如此的惱人
沉沉昏昏
茫茫迷迷
在痛哭流涕與嘔心瀝血間翻滾
毫無章法，不合邏輯
如同平衡在細針上的巨石
使人疑惑，令人膽寒

Miscellaneous-1

Sickness
Sleepily dizzy
Dizzily Sleepy
The fever dreams are always so annoying
Dizzily Sleepy
Sleepily dizzy
Twist and turn in pain, tears, snot, and heartache
Without reason, without logic
Like a boulder balancing on the tip of a needle
Confusing and frightening

旅途—黃金國的邀請函 Journey - Invitation to El Dorado　65×80 cm　acrylic on canvas　2016

旅途—黃金國的邀請函

天空

大地

青草

白雲

黃金的光輝

追思，夢想，那閃耀的時代

黃金鄉的大門永遠為你而開

手持邀請函的你，何不踏上光輝的旅程？

Journey - Invitation to El Dorado

Heaven

And Earth

The Grass

And the Clouds

The shine of gold

Remiss, dream, that bright shining time

The door of El Dorado shall always open

To you who holds the invitation, why not begin that bright journey?

旅途—大漠商港 Journey - Dessert Trading Port　65×80 cm　oil on canvas　2016

旅途—大漠商港

賣香料！賣香料！世上最好的香料！

哎年輕人要買香料嗎？我這人的香料應有盡有，煮飯用的，治病用的，要是你有興趣的話我甚至娛樂用的都…

啥？彩帶？哦你是說"魂帶"啊。呵呵年輕人這是你第一次來凱紮菲吧？哈哈我知道在你們外地人看來估計有點奇怪，但這可是咱們這兒的傳統

什麼？哈哈看不出你還挺有好奇心的啊。我是不介意跟你解釋啦但你要知道，我家裡那口子兒的很，要給她瞧見我和個路人瞎聊天那我屁股得挨踹啊！當然，要是你是個付錢的客人的話那我和你聊兩句也理所當…

嗯？哦我當然有龍椒粉啊你要多少？好您等我一會兒……好咧一共是 10 克楞。多謝惠顧！請問您還有什麼需要嗎？

哦對了對了對了，剛剛正說到魂帶呢。你可知道在飛空船發明之前要跨越這人沙漠可是件要命的差事。沙丘瞬息萬變，數不清的人在裡頭迷失了方向然後就沒能活著出來。傳說要是你死在沙漠裡頭，你的靈魂就得永遠迷失在沙海裡。

什麼？您問這和彩帶有什麼關係？哎呀客人聽故事您得有點耐心啊！想當然而沒人想被困在沙漠裡永世不得超生，所以他們就會把身上的衣服剪一塊下來交給祭祀們祈福，然後把那塊布高高掛起來。這樣萬一他們死在沙漠裡頭了，他們的靈魂就能看見被祈福的布條從而找到回家的路。一代代的旅人，商人，探險家們都把他們的布條掛在了這裡，很快的就沒地方掛了。而且咱們也不能把老的布條給拿下來，畢竟誰知道那些人的魂魄是回來了沒有。所以我們的祖先就決定把那些布條全縫起來像這樣一起掛著。哈？你問我到底靈不靈？哎呀客人我怎麼知道啊？我又沒在沙漠裡死過！

這年頭有了飛空船跨越沙漠要方便多了。但縫魂帶已經成了這裡的傳統。且不論它是不是真能引領幽魂回家，所有曾經來到這座城市的人們都留下了他們的痕跡，而且會永遠在我們頭上飛揚。這不也挺好嗎？

哦？客人這就要走了？謝謝惠顧下次再來啊！

Journey - Dessert Trading Port

Spices! Spices! The best spices you could find in the world!

Hey you, young man, wanna buy some spices! I've got spices good for cooking and for medicine. I've even got stuff for recreational use if you're into that kind of stuff...

Hmm? Ribbons? Oh you mean the Soul Ties! Haha this must be your first visit to Kel-Zaphil huh? Yeah I know, it must be pretty strange to you outsiders. But it's a tradition of ours.

What's that? Haha you're quite a curious one aren't you? Well I'd love to talk but my wife will kick my ass if she catches me chit-chatting to some random traveler. If only you're a paying customer then I'd be more than happy to....

Hmm? Yes? Oh of course we've got Dragon pepper! How much do you need? Alright just give me a moment....... and... that would be 10 Kellem sir. Thank you very much.... Is there anything else you need?

Hmm? Oh yes the Soul Ties! Well you see once upon a time before the airships were invented, people have to cross the Great Dessert on foot. Needless to say that it's a dangerous ordeal and many people got lost in the ever changing dunes and were never seen again, and it's said that those people who got lost in the dessert would turn into wandering spirits, cursed to walk the dunes forever.

What's that have to do with the ribbons? Patience sir. I'm getting at it! Obviously people don't wanna get lost and wander the dunes forever, so before they enter the dessert they'd cut a piece of cloth from their clothing and a priest with bestow blessing upon it. They'd then hang the cloth high up in the air so if their souls were ever lost in the dessert, their clothes would guide them back home. Generations upon generations of travelers, traders, and adventurers left their Soul ties here and soon we ran out of places to hang them, and it's not like we can throw away the old ones cause, you know, people's souls are tethered to them. So our ancestors decided to sew them all together and hang them up like this. Hmm? What's that? Does it actually work? How would I know dear sir, I've never been dead in the dessert and need a Soul tie to guide me back home.

Anyway nowadays it's easy to cross the dessert with airships, but it has become a tradition for anyone crossing to add their cloth to the existing tie. Regardless of whether it could guide lost souls or not, everyone who'd came to this city left their mark and would forever be part of this place. That itself is a pretty nice thing don't you think?

Hmm? Going already? That's a pity. Well it's nice doing business with ya, stop by anytime!

旅途—廢城 Journey - Ruins　　65×80 cm　　oil on canvas　　2016

旅途─廢城

月，懸掛與天際，看盡了國家文明的興衰

光，閃爍在水面，映照著人去樓空的殘骸

古老的廢墟畫上了銀色的妝　　無頭的天使敘述著亡國的殤

夜晚的冷風滲入旅人的殘軀　　孤單的火把見證過去的榮光

空洞的廟堂，彷彿還迴盪著信徒誠心或狂信的詠唱

一廂情願的愛與信仰，在天地流轉間被緩緩磨滅

夜霧掩蓋了逝去的傷痛

藤蔓纏繞了殿堂的樑柱

青苔覆蓋了聖者的長袍

旅人疑問：望向過去的雙目可否找到一絲光芒？

夜晚回答：答案永遠在黑暗的前方。

Journey - Ruins

The moon, hanging high above, have witnessed the rise and fall of men

The light, flickering on water, reflecting the ruins of what's left

Old relics have put on a silver make up

Headless angels telling stories of how the nation fell

The cold night wind seeped into the traveler's frail form

But a lone torch now, witnessing the glory that's long gone

Fanatic chanting still lingered in the empty halls

Wishful love wishful faith, has been grind down by the flow of time

The night mist has covered the pain of loss

Vines crawling up the pillars of palaces

Moss covering the robes of saints

The traveler wondered: Can eyes looking into the past find light?

The night replied: The answer is always beyond the darkness.

旅途—與大海的偶遇 Journey - Chance encounter with the Sea　　65×80 cm　　oil on canvas　　2017

旅途—與大海的偶遇

他以為他死定了

鑑於剛發生的事這個結論似乎是理所當然。畢竟有誰能在跨洋的飛空船爆炸後沒降落傘也沒任何守護魔法的狀況下從天墜海還能存活呢？

但他活下來了，毫髮無傷且呼吸順暢，但奇妙的是他正身處水面下。據旅人所知他的祖先並沒有半魚人或兩棲類的血脈，他看著氣泡隨著他的吐息緩緩浮向水面，而當他吸氣時他明確的能感覺到空氣充滿著他的肺葉。這完全不合常理，但卻正是這不合理在維持著他的生命。當然比起漸漸沉入無底深淵，他更希望能夠早點回到陸地上。

但深淵並非無底，很快旅人發現他逐漸接近海床 而眼前的光景使他驚嘆不已。美麗的珊瑚礁與色彩繽紛的魚群吸引了他的注意，突然，他發現一隻發光的紅眼與他對視。而下一秒他的身體開始不住的顫抖。

那紅眼不止一隻。

成千上萬的紅眼突然在海中浮現，好似海流本身突然有了生命。旅人驚恐的看著深藍的海水中漸漸浮現成一個類似女人的形體，無數發光的紅眼從它，她的身上窺視而來。

旅人被恐懼所震懾讓他不敢動彈，就算他能動他也沒辦法改善現況。本能的他意識到他正面對著一個難以想像的古老與強人的存在。或許她是傳說中古老神明的一份子？又或者她是某種完全不同的東西？旅人只得靜靜的承受那無數的視線。

她來的突然，她也去的突然。無數的眼睛與她龐大的形體很快的溶解在海中，而隨著旅人開始升向海面他感覺意識漸漸模糊。等他回過神來他已經被沖到了岸邊躺在一片沙灘上。看著頂上的藍天他回想起方才的經歷不由得自問：到底發生了什麼？他是做了場夢，還是溺水時看到了幻覺？一切都是如此的超乎常理。

當然，他早就將所謂常理丟出窗外了。

Journey - Chance encounter with the Sea

He thought he was dead.

Given the circumstances it wasn't a bad assessment. After all, how could he survive when the airship he was on exploded during a transcontinental flight, then fell from the sky into the middle of the ocean without a parachute nor any form of protection rune or magic?

And yet here he was, living and breathing, which was also something quite bizarre since he was deep under water. Last time he checked the traveler was of pure human lineage and had no blood relatives who were of fish or amphibian descent. He looked at the bubbles that left his nose and mouth in wonder and bemusement, and as he took a deep breath he could feel his lungs filled with the precious substance which kept land creatures like him alive. Something was wrong, though given that it was this wrongness which was keeping him alive, the traveler wasn't about to complain. That being said, he would very much want to get back on dry land instead of being dragged into what seemed to be a bottomless abyss.

But of course, the ocean was not bottomless. Soon the traveler found himself approaching the ocean floor and he was surprised by the fantastical sight in front of his eyes: beautiful coral reefs with swarms of colorful fish swimming. For a moment he was mesmerized by the beauty of the sight but suddenly a cold shiver came up his spine when his eyes met with a shining red eye starring back.

And then there were more.

Hundreds, thousands of big red eyes emerged out of nowhere as if the ocean currents themselves had come alive. To the traveler's horror water slowly began to take "shape", despite how ridiculous it may seem, the blue dark waters down the bottom of the ocean began to form into a massive, vaguely humanoid form, with the countless eyes peaking from all over its, her, body.

The traveler was petrified and couldn't even move a finger, not that the ability to move would've improved his situation. Instinctively he knew he was in the presence of something unimaginably old and powerful. Could she be one of the gods that people told tales about? Or perhaps she was something completely different? For a while he just floated there as the countless red eyes kept their gazes fixed on him.

Then as abruptly as she appeared, the red eyes faded and the waters lost its form. The ocean returned to normal and the traveler found himself quickly floating up and he felt his consciousness quickly fading. By the time he woke up he was washed up shore and laying on a sandy beach. Looking up towards the blue sky he thought about the experience he just had. What in the heaven's name just happened? Was it just a dream or hallucination he had while drowning or did that really happen? None of what happened made sense.

But of course, he'd thrown common sense out of the window long ago.

隨筆 -2

大海總是讓我困惑不已

我知道海洋是生命之源，但上億年的演化給了我們呼吸空氣的肺與行走在大地上的雙腳。

那人類有事沒事又跑到海裡是想怎樣？

他們不知道海裡充滿了危險嗎？

尖牙，毒刺，更別說沒有空氣。

在我看來，大海顯然不接受退貨，壓根不想要我們回去。

但為什麼那麼多人愛游泳，潛水，探索那黑暗的角落？

或許自找麻煩是人性的一部分？

又或許是某種歸巢本能作祟？

或許是大海在呼喚著我們？如同母親在喊子女回家吃飯？

她渴望著，期盼著她的兒女回家？這樣她才能將他們悶死在溫柔鄉中？

無論如何我選擇潔身自愛，免得發現深淵正凝視著我們。

Miscellaneous-2

There's something about the Ocean that bothers me

I mean yes, I know that the Ocean is the source of all life and all.

But millions of years of evolution gave us lungs and legs for a reason right?

Then why on Earth would people want to get back into the water?

Don't they know that the Ocean is filled with danger?

Sharp teeth, poisonous stings, not to mention the lack of air.

Seems to me that the Ocean had a strict no return policy. Clearly it doesn't want us there.

Then why are we so eager to swim, to dive, to explore its darkest depths?

Perhaps it's human nature to poke our noses into places that we don't belong?

Or perhaps it's some sort of homing instinct? An Oedipus complex on an existential scale?

Or perhaps it's the other way around? Perhaps the sea calls to us? Like a mother calling her child for dinner,

Longingly, lovingly, for her child to return? So that she may snuff your life out in her loving embrace?

In any case I prefer to stay at a healthy distance, or the abyss might just stare back.

旅途—茶會 Journey - Tea party　65×80 cm　oil on canvas　2016

茶會

　　旅人發現自己身處一座美麗的花園中，被整齊典雅的樹木與花叢環繞。雖然周遭的環境平靜安詳，旅人的內心卻是緊張不已，畢竟他完全沒有如何來到此地的記憶。他也不記得有服用過什麼會造成幻覺的藥品，至少沒有自願服用過。

　　「啊！終於來了個客人！」突然旅人聽見身後傳來說話聲。當他轉過身時眼前的景象讓他大吃一驚。一個頭戴金冠，身穿紅袍好似半人半蟲的巨大生物。用著甜蜜而溫暖的聲音它笑道：「來，請坐。」

　　「坐？」旅人納悶道，但下一秒他發現自己坐在一張柔軟舒適的椅子上，以前的桌子擺滿了各式糕點與甜品。不知何時他手上已經拿著一杯冒著熱氣的紅茶。不由自主的他將茶杯帶到唇邊，高級的茶香充斥了他的口腔，溫暖了他的臟腑。他頓時覺得心平氣和，安詳快樂。

　　「感覺好點了嗎？」那奇怪的生物問道。

　　「啊…對，好多了。」旅人回答。他看著周圍美麗的庭院說道：「這地方挺不錯的。」

　　「你喜歡就好。我可是花了不少功夫打理呢！」那生物回答。它很快就注意到了旅人看向桌上餐點的視線並說：「盡量吃不必客氣。」

　　「啊不用……我很飽。」旅人回答道，雖然他全身上下一切的感官讓他覺得放鬆安心，但腦中僅留的一絲警覺與理性讓他不得不防範這怪生物的熱情。他緊張的問道：「你是誰？這是什麼地方？我是怎麼到這裡來的？」

　　那生物蠕動著接近了桌子並拿起了水煙管，它深吸了一口氣後吐出了一團厚實的煙霧。它輕笑了數聲後說：「你可以叫我蟲后，這是我的花園。至於你是怎麼來到這的……」它停頓了一下接著說道：「你可是自己走進來的。難道你不記得嗎？」

　　「自己走進？…不…我不記得了……」旅人納悶的嘀咕。

　　「既然忘了就忘了吧。重要的是開心就好～」蟲后一邊吞雲吐霧的說。

　　「你說的也對……」旅人嘀咕道。雖然他的情況實在是太詭異，但身處蟲后的花園實在是讓他感到太安全，祥和了。桌上的茶點讓他流連忘返，很快他就忘記了時間。他到底在哪兒呆了多久？

他感覺好似只過了幾分鐘，但又像他已經在那坐了好幾個小時，好幾天，幾年，甚至幾十年。但旅人並不介意，至少一開始他不。但漸漸的他的心開始躁動，好似他的五臟六腑在發癢，飢渴，鞭策著他離開這個安全和樂的地方。離開去哪？回到那充滿痛苦，失望與孤獨的路途？回到那不見終點，非常有可能會葬送他的旅程？

旅人長嘆了一口氣並他站起身來。他看向依舊安然自得的蟲后說道：「多謝您的款待，但我該離開了。」

「哦？這麼快就要走？你確定不想呆久一點？」蟲后轉向旅人，此時她隱藏在金色前髮下的雙眸發出了一陣奇特但溫柔的光芒。不知為何旅人心知蟲后想把他留在此地並非出自惡意，而是出自憐憫之心。旅人搖了搖頭答道：「謝謝你，但我得繼續趕路。麻煩告訴我離開的路嗎？」

蟲后沉默了一瞬，但很快她又露出了笑容：「這你不必擔心。你已經離開了。」

突然旅人從夢中甦醒。昨夜升起的營火早已熄滅，他從雜草與毯子做成了臨時床鋪上爬起他放眼向眼前的草原望去，正好看見太陽正從地平線緩緩上升。

Tea party

The traveler found himself standing in the middle of a beautiful garden, surrounded by bushes, trees and flowers which was well maintained in an orderly, and elegant fashion. Contrary to the calm surroundings the traveler was on high alert, since he had no memory how or why he was there in the first place. He was sure that he had not taken any substances which would explain this gap in his memory, at least not willingly.

"Ah....finally, a guest!" Suddenly a voice came from behind the traveler, he turned around and was in awe by the being in front of his eyes, a massive worm like creature with the upper body resembling a woman, it had a golden crown on its head and was wearing a bright red cape. Speaking in a sweet, and gentle voice the creature smiled: "Come on please, have a seat."

"A seat? A seat where?" The traveler muttered but the next moment he found himself sitting in front of a large table filled with all kinds of cakes, sweets, and desserts. The chair was rather soft and comfortable. He was surprised to find a teacup in his own hands and as if entranced he brought the cup to his lips without a second thought, the taste of top grade tea flavored with milk and sugar stimulated his taste buds and almost immediately he felt himself shrouded in an euphoric sense of clam, ease, tranquility and happiness.

"Feeling better?" The strange creature asked.

"Ye...Yes... I think so..." The traveler replied. Looking around the beautiful garden he smiled: "It's a nice place you've got here."

"Glad that you like it. I worked quite hard to keep it this way." The creature smiled as it noticed the travelers gaze which had fell upon the food on the table and added: "Go ahead, take whatever you want."

"Oh... it's quite alright I'm full." The traveler lied, despite his entire being feeling at ease and trusting, the shred of caution and reason compelled him to reject the creature's invitation. He asked hesitantly: "Who are you and where am I? How did I end up here?"

The creature squirmed a bit closer to the table as it picked up the pipe of the hookah, it took a deep breath from the pipe and blew out a thick gust of thick smoke. Chuckling joyfully it then said: "You may call me the Worm Queen and this is my garden. As for how you ended up here...." It paused for a moment and said: "You walked into my garden yourself. Don't you remember?"

"No I... don't..." The traveler muttered.

"Well it doesn't really matter does it? What's important for you now is to enjoy yourself~" the Worm Queen said before blowing another puff of smoke.

"I suppose.... you are right...." the traveler muttered. Despite the strange circumstances somehow being here in the Worm Queen's garden just made him feel... safe, happy. He enjoyed a wonderful time drinking hot tea and eating all the sweet snacks on the table and it didn't take long for him to lose track of time. Just how long he had stayed there? Hours? Days? Years or even decades? The traveler couldn't tell, and frankly, the traveler didn't care, at least for a while. But eventually something buried deep inside him began to stir, an inexplicable itch, hunger, a craving of sorts, something that compelled him to leave this place, and for what? For a journey filled with torment, disappointment, and solitude? For a journey with no end in sight, a journey which more than likely would end in utter disaster?

With a heavy sigh the traveler put down the teacup and stood up from his comfortable chair. He said with renewed conviction in his voice: "Thank you for your hospitality Worm Queen, but I must go."

"Oh! Leaving so soon? You sure you don't want to stay for a bit longer?" The worm queen asked as a gentle light flickered under the thick blond hair that covered much of her face. Traveler could tell that the Worm Queen wished to keep him there not out of malice, but out of mercy. Shaking his head the traveler said: "Thank you, but I need to get back on the road. Mind showing me the way out?"

The Worm Queen stayed still for a moment but soon she smiled: "Don't worry my dear guest, you're already out."

The next moment the traveler woke up. The campfire he'd made last night had died out during the night and as he got up from his makeshift bed of grass and blankets he looked towards the grass fields in front of him, with the sun slowly rising above the horizon.

旅途—在龍骨之下 Journey - Under the Dragon's Bones　91×117 cm　oil on canvas　2020

旅途—在龍骨之下

很久很久以前，眾神在這片大地上仰首跨步

祂們的步伐使地面崩裂，祂們的聲音讓天空顫抖。祂們隨性的統治著這個世界，從不注意在祂們腳下苟延殘喘的弱小生命。

有一天巨龍們從星空降臨。它們的眼比太陽更耀眼，它們的牙比峭壁更銳利，它們的爪比山脈更雄偉，它們的身軀比群島還冗長。巨龍與眾神在地上，在海裡，在空中廝殺，將世界化為一片廢墟。它們腳下的弱小生命們沒辦法只能無助的祈禱戰爭結束，而那天終究是到來了。當它們從藏身的洞穴中探出頭腦時它們發現了滿目瘡痍的世界，但龍與眾神卻不見了。

歲月流逝，那些弱小的生命們茁壯成長，他們自稱為「人類」並征服了一度荒蕪的大地。他們忘記了眾神，忘記了巨龍，忘記了那驚天動地的戰爭，他們忘記了抱頭鼠竄的過去並成為了這個世界的主人。但有一天他們發現了它，一具巨龍的屍骨。他們被巨龍所震懾，在龍骨的倒影下他們不由自主的向巨龍頂禮膜拜。巨龍即使身死，它的遺骸依舊呢喃著它的偉大，它的力量。

巨龍的謠傳很快在人群中傳播引得更多人前來一睹究竟。一個小露營地很快變成了村莊，小鎮，城市乃至一個王國。統治者們宣稱自己為巨龍永恆意志的先知，貴族與僧侶以官僚體系與宗教儀式支持著王權，商人們販賣者他們宣稱是從巨龍骸骨提取而來的萬靈藥，而嚮導們則帶領遊客們登高從而一望龍骨的神奇。如同環繞在屍體邊的蒼蠅般他們在龍骨之下繁衍生息，沒人真的關心那死去的生靈到底怎麼看待它身邊的鬧劇。

摘選自偽經：黎明書

Journey - Under the Dragon's Bones

Once upon a time, the Gods walked this earth.

Their strides shattered the ground and their voices shook the skies. They ruled the world with careless abandon and cared little for the small creatures that lived beneath their heels.

And then the Dragons came from the stars, massive creatures with eyes brighter than suns and teeth sharper than cliffs, their claws larger than mountains and bodies longer than archipelagos. Dragons and Gods did battle on the land, in the sea, and in the air, they devastated the world and all the small creatures could do was hide and pray for the battle to end, and one day, it did. As those creatures emerged from their hideouts they saw the scars of the battle everywhere, but not a single living Dragon nor God was to be found.

Years, centuries, millenia latter, the small creatures now calling themselves "men" had spread across the once barren land. They've forgotten the gods, the dragons, the battles that shock the earth and heavens. They've forgotten the past when they cowered in fear underground and had became masters of the land. Then one day they found it, the remains of a Great Dragon and stood in awe at its majesty. As they stood in the shadow of the dragon's bones they couldn't help but kneel and worship, for even in death, the Dragon whispered its greatness, its power.

Those adventurers spread the word of their discovery and soon more and more people came to bear witness of the remains. What began as small camps became a village, a town, a city and eventually a kingdom. Rulers claimed themselves to be the prophet of the great dragon and spoke for its eternal spirit, nobles and clergy supported their claims through bureaucracy and rituals, merchants sold what they claimed to be fragments of the dragon's bones as elixirs which treats all illnesses, and tour guides lead curious travelers on the many hills nearby to watch the remains in its full glory. Like flies on a corpse they thrived under the Dragon's bones, caring little for what the dead creature may actually think of the whole charade.

Extract from the pseudepigrapha: Book of Dawn

人像

　　長久以來人體一直是西方藝術中十分重要的主題。古希臘的藝術家們將人體視為最純粹的藝術形式之一，他們視科學，哲學，藝術為一體，並試圖通過表現自然完美的人體進而探討某種超越俗世的美麗。即便對人體的刻畫在中世紀所謂的黑暗時代暫緩，隨著文藝復興這一追求也隨著復甦至現在。「完整」的人體象徵著美麗，完美，甚至神聖性，那想當然因各種原因而變得「異常」或「不完整」的人體則會讓人恐懼或作嘔。

　　但對完美肉體的嚮往幾乎與對其相對面的癡迷一般古老。英語中怪誕（Grotesque）一詞源自於義大利語的洞穴 grotto，因發現被埋入地下的古羅馬皇帝尼祿的宮殿中的那些人獸交雜的怪異裝飾 Grotesque 一詞成為了這類裝飾的名稱。更別說在所有的文化與文明的傳說故事裡都能見到的那些半人半獸的奇特生物，比如米諾陶洛斯，人馬，人魚，哈比，甚至亞伯拉罕諸教中所描繪的異形的高階天使。當然將人體「去完美化」的方法不僅僅是將其「怪誕化」。藝術家在發展抽象藝術的過程中也對人體進行了大膽的改變，比如省略去五官，肢體，甚至將人體簡化到了最基本的剪影。

或許有人會說對人體細節的省略是對追求某種純粹的，純淨的形體或精神的結果。但我必須問：為什麼移除個體特徵能創造出這所謂的純淨？或許並不是那所謂的純淨，而是那相對於正常，「完美」肉體而言的「欠缺」或「不完美」吸引了我們的眼球？那我們又是為什麼被怪誕，被不完美所吸引？當一個人體無眼，無鼻，無口，無耳，無臉，無頭，無指，無手，無腳，無足，無性，甚至毫無器官時那又代表了什麼？當人體的細節被移除時會產生什麼樣的可能性？反之當人體的器官增生，變化，與有機物與無機物融合時又會給予我們什麼樣的啟發？

　　因此我創作了這些人像，將人體抽象，誇張，延展與變化。他們不僅是對人性體的探索，更是對感官與心靈邊界的探索。可以說他們是我思考與感覺的面相或化身。但這種自我滿足式的荒誕探索對世間有什麼價值呢？在我看來我的感性絕不獨特，而通過分享我的探索我希望能夠在觀者心中產生某種共鳴。如果我能做到這點的話對我來說就足夠了。

Portrait

The human body has always been an important subject matter in western art, which roots can be traced all the way back to the time of antiquity when the ancient Greeks saw the depiction of human body as one of the purest form of art. With science, philosophy, and art seen as one and the same, ancient Greeks sought to pursuit a transcending beauty of humanity through the depiction of the body, most often nude in order to show its most natural form. Though interrupted by the dark ages, such fascination of the body reemerged during the renaissance and continued till this day. With the "whole" body being associated with ideals of beauty, perfection, and even divinity, it's no wonder that the "abnormal" or "incomplete" body, whether due to illness or injury, would usually result in fear, repulsion, or both from people.

Yet the fascination towards perfect bodily beauty was almost as old as the fascination towards its contraries. For instance the term Grotesque originated from the Italian word grotto. Originally meaning caves it became associated to the strange and bizarre decorations in Roman ruins when Nero's Domus Aurea was discovered. Not to mention the countless half-man, half-beast creatures and beings you could find in legend of almost every culture and nations：minotaurs, centaurs, mermaids, harpies and so on, even high-ranking angels depicted in various Abrahamic religions. But of course, there are more ways to make the body "imperfect", as artists in the process of abstraction omitted facial features, body parts, reduced the human body to its most basic silhouette.

While one may argue that the omission of bodily features in abstract art was the result of seeking some sort of purity in form, and perhaps spirit, one then have to ask the question: why does the lack of identifiers create purity? Or perhaps it's not the supposed "purity" of those forms which attracted our eyes, but the blatant imperfection in comparison to a "whole" body? Why does the imperfection of the human body fascinate artists so much? What does it mean to be eyeless, noseless, mouthless, earless, faceless, headless, fingerless, handless, toeless, legless, sexless, or utterly organless? What possibilities are created when organs are omitted from the human body in art? On the other hand, human bodies also go through other kinds of transformation in art, with their body parts Multiplied, morphed, combined with organic or inorganic matters. What insights can we learn from such transformations?

It is with these reasons that I created these "portraits". They can be seen as abstraction or reduction of the human form, but also its expansion, elaboration and aberration. They're not just an exploration into the possibilities of the human form, but also an exploration of the possibilities of our sensibilities and mental horizons. In a way they're my different facade of my thoughts and feelings, or in another word, my avatars. But what's such self-indulgence into the absurd worth to the rest of the world? It is my opinion that my sensibilities are by no means unique, and by sharing my explorations I attempt to evoke something that perhaps could resonate in the viewers as well. If I am successful in achieving that then it would be more than enough.

延展中的宇宙 Expanding Universe　　130×194 cm　　acrylic on canvas　　2015

延展中的宇宙

人的臂膀，即便踏上高山
也捉不到慧星的尾巴
人的雙腳，縱使耗盡一生
也回不去夢中的故鄉
世界的盡頭
宇宙的邊界
實際的路途遙不可及
但想像的翅膀能超越時空

Expanding universe

Even atop of a mountain, a man's arm
Cannot reach the tails of comets
Even exhausting a whole lifetime, a man's legs
Cannot return him to the home seen in dreams
The ends of the world
The edges of the universe
The real path stayed unexplored
But the wings of imagination could traverse time and space

人格疏離 Personality Fragmentation　72.5×60cm　acrylic on canvas　2015

人格疏離

眼前的現實似乎遙不可及
緊握的五指卻陌生的難以忍受
一瞬間的迷茫
一瞬間的疏離
你是誰？
你是我嗎？
還是他？
亦或是她？
還是他它她他他它她它？

Personality Fragmentation

The reality in front of my eyes seemed so unteachable
Yet the feeling of clenched fists felt unbearably unfamiliar
Momentary confusion
Momentary distance
Who are you?
Are you me?
Or him?
Or her?
Or him her it her him it her him?

流離 Astray　72.5×60 cm　acrylic on canvas　2015

流離

「家」是一個許多人認為理所當然，而對於很多人卻是遙不可及的概念。

「家」不僅僅是一天過後躺下沉睡的地方，那是個人心靈的寄託，

感情的依靠，那甚至是族群，血脈，文化傳承的所在。

而沒有家的人則如同無根的樹木，飄搖不定，漸漸凋零。

個人的境遇，時代的洪流，都可能讓人失去他的「家」，

讓他們流離失所，苦不堪言。即使回到故地，物是人非，滄海桑田，

心中的家早已不知去向。

Astray

"Home" is something many took for granted, and for many others unreachable.

"Home" is not simply the place where you sleep at the end of the day,

it is the harbor of your heart, anchor for your emotions,

even the pillar to which family, blood, and culture lineage was built upon.

A person without home is like a tree without roots, wavering, withering.

Both individual experience and the current of the epoch could make someone lose their "home",

make them astray, in pain.

Even by chance they managed to return to the physical location,

as things change with time the home in their heart might have been long gone.

啊 Ah　72.5×60 cm　acrylic on canvas　2015

啊

啊啊 啊啊 啊啊 啊啊 啊啊 啊啊 啊啊 啊啊 啊啊

啊啊 啊啊 啊啊 啊啊 啊啊 啊啊 啊啊 啊啊 啊啊 啊啊

啊啊 啊啊 啊啊 啊啊 啊啊 啊啊

啊啊 啊啊 啊啊 啊啊 啊啊 啊啊

啊啊 啊啊 啊啊 啊啊 啊啊 啊啊 啊啊 啊啊 啊啊 啊啊 啊啊 啊啊 啊啊 啊啊

啊啊 啊啊 啊啊 啊啊 啊啊 啊啊 啊啊 啊啊 啊啊 啊啊

啊啊 啊啊 啊啊 啊啊 啊啊 啊啊

Ah

AAAAAAAAAAAAAAH

AAAAAAAAAAAAAAAAAAAAAH

AAAAHHH

AAAHHHH

AAAAAAAAAAAAAAAAAAAH

AAAAAAAAAAAAAAAAAAH

AAAAAAAAAH

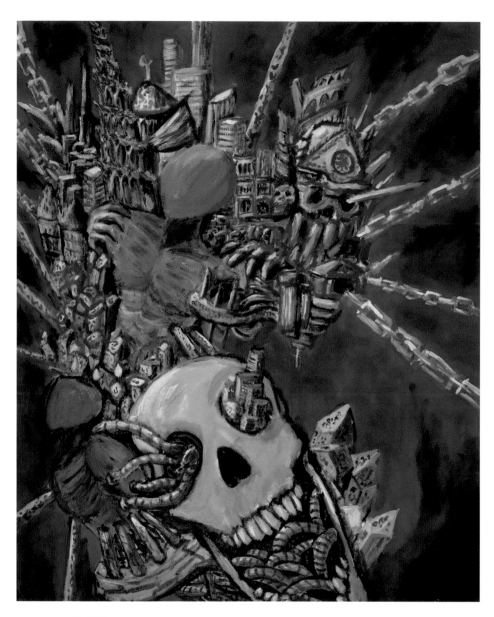

黃金獄 Golden Infernal　　100×80 cm　　acrylic on canvas　　2015

黃金獄

黃金是高貴的象徵
同時也是慾望的象徵
玉樓宮闕是榮耀成就的具現，
但俗世浮華何嘗不是通往喜樂的障礙？
然而財富與名聲本身沒有價值，是人心賦予了它們價值，
而也是人心將自己困在慾望的煉獄之中。
到頭來天堂，地獄，只在一念之間。

Golden Infernal

Gold symbolizes nobility
But also of desire
Lavish palaces are glory solidified
But aren't they also obstacle on the way towards happiness and peace?
Wealth and have no value, it's our hearts that bestowed it
So it's our hearts that chain us in infernal
Heaven or hell, all in a thought

煩 Frustration　72.5×60 cm　acrylic on canvas　2015

煩

世間充滿了種種事物
好事
壞事
美事
醜事
奇妙的事
糟糕的事
然後還有煩人的事
當電腦當機毀了你的心血的時候
當你小腳趾踢到櫃子的時候
當蚊子在耳邊輾轉不肯離去的時候
當你看著空白的稿紙發呆的時候
煩惱，我的老友啊
你讓我氣得血脈沸騰

Frustration

The world is filled with many things
Good things
Bad things
Beautiful things
Ugly things
Wonderful things
Terrible things
And then there are the frustrating things
When the computer froze and cost you hours of work
When you hit your toe on the edge of the wardrobe
When the mosquitoes keep buzzing around your ear
When your brain went blank when starring at your work
Frustration, my old friend.
You make my veins pop, blood boil

影（本我） Shadow (Id)　91×117 cm　oil on canvas　2018

影（本我）

陰影是身體受光而生的空缺。
它雖形似身體，且與之相連，但欠缺了太多身體的細節。
有光就有影，外在的光芒產生了陰影，
那內在的光芒，靈魂，思想，人格的光芒的影子又在哪裡？
我們的耳眼口鼻身體髮膚何嘗能夠表現出內在的喜怒哀樂，愛恨情仇？
如此這般，難道身體不就是靈魂的陰影嗎？
讓陰影真正的成為身體，乃至心靈的映照，
讓本我，自我，超我從影子中流淌而出化為具型。
慾望也好，愛憎也罷，都讓它張牙舞爪的綻放吧！

Shadow (Id)

Shadow is the blank space left from the light
It looks like the body and is attached to it, but lacking much detail
Where there is light, there is shadow, as one was the source of the other
But if so, then where did the light within, the light of one's soul, mind, and personality casts its shadow?
How could our ears eyes mouths noses flesh and hair truly reflect our emotions, our love, hate and desires?
Aren't our bodies but shadows of our hearts?
Then let the shadow show our true nature, show our inner self
Let id, ego and super-ego flow out of the shadow and take form
Let desire, love and hate bloom wild and flourish

飛天 Apsaras 91×117 cm oil on canvas 2017

飛天

天人夢，愚眾祈
睡浮無明
萬古逝，星辰熄
神人盡塵

Apsaras

The Devas dreams as the masses pray
Asleep, adrift, unaware and uncaring
Aeons pass and stars fade
Both gods and men wither to dust

進化 Evolution　　117×91 cm　　oil on canvas　　2018

進化

Evolution

有時自然會拿走你的雙眼
有時生命會給你一對翅膀
有時宇宙決定你需要多一雙臂膀
有時上天下旨你該試著下水一遊

進化存在於存在的每一個層面
每個細胞都得為了生存而奮鬥
變強
變弱
變肥
變瘦
踏上冒險的旅途
種下不動的深根
尋得快樂
陷入悲傷
生命即是變化
未必會變好，但永不停歇
我們有追求快樂的權利
但沒人保證我們真能找到
僅僅想感覺快樂的話吃點藥就行
但要活得有意義則更有挑戰性

所以進化吧，即便前方等待的是條死路
但總比駐足不前要強

At times, nature take away your eyes
At times, life gives you wings
At times, the universe decide that you should have an extra pair of limbs
At times, gods decreed that maybe you should give swimming a try

Evolution is written in every facet of our existence
As every single cell in your body strife to survive
To get strong
To go weak
To grow fat
To get lean
To go on great adventures
To be rooted at one place
To be happy
Or to be sad
To live, is to change
Not necessarily for the better, but never the same
We have the right to pursuit happiness
But none said we should ever find it
All you need is some narcotics to feel joy
But to have meaning, that's the real challenge

So change, evolve,
though what awaits you could be a dead end
But it is still better than the alternative

綠眼的怪物 Green-eyed monster　117×91 cm　oil on canvas　2018

綠眼的怪物

啊，主帥，您要留心嫉妒啊！
那是一個綠眼妖魔，誰做了它的犧牲，誰就要受它的玩弄！

奧賽羅 ，1604， 莎士比亞

Green eyed monster

"O, beware, my lord, of jealousy;
It is the green-eyed monster which doth mock
The meat it feeds on."

Othello, 1604, Shakespeare

矗立 Stand　117×91 cm　oil on canvas　2018

矗立

不退不讓
昂首而立
讓風刮
讓雨下
讓天塌
我無妨
人皆需立足之地
那就別退縮分毫

Stand

Stand your ground
Standing proud
Be it wind
Or the rain
The sky could fall
And I don't care
We all need a place
So stand your ground

舞動 Dance　　117×91 cm　　oil on canvas　　2017

舞動

是什麼讓我們的身體隨著音樂舞動？
想著也奇怪，這樣的行為對物種的繁衍看似沒有任何幫助
但我們還是跳著，慢舞，快舞，在悲傷時，在歡喜時，冷靜的，熱情的跳著
或許音樂有某種根源性的，古老的特質？
某種碰觸到我們所處現實本質的力量？
或許世間存在某種超常的存在，
正彈奏宇宙作為祂的樂器
以時空做弦，生命為樂？
或許當我們隨著音樂起舞之時，
我們也能稍微碰觸到那原始的真實？

Dance

What compels our body to move when listening to music?
It seems odd, given that such a reaction seemed counterproductive to a creature's survival
And yet we move, we dance, slowly, quickly, sadly, happily, soberly and passionately
Perhaps there was something more fundamental,
more primordial to the concept of music?
Something that tapped into the very fabric of reality and existence itself?
Perhaps there is a divine being beyond our understanding,
playing the universe as its instrument
With time and space as its strings, and life itself as its music?
Perhaps by playing and dancing to music ourselves,
we touch upon such primordial truth if just on its most rudimentary form?

超越者 The Ascended　　117×91 cm　　oil on canvas　　2018

超越者

詛咒這副血肉之軀

效率差 不優雅

不重要 不完美

我多想脫下這臭皮囊

變的偉大 超越自我

人體的局限灼燒著我的心靈

存在的桎梏讓我癲狂

伸展 開裂

繁殖 變異

變化 昇華

The Ascended

To hell with this flesh and blood

Inefficient

Inelegant

Insignificant

Imperfect

Oh how I wished to shed this mortal coil

To become greater

To transcend

The limitations of human form scorch my mind

The restrictions of my existence drive me insane

Reach out

Splinter

Multiply

Mutate

Transform

Ascend

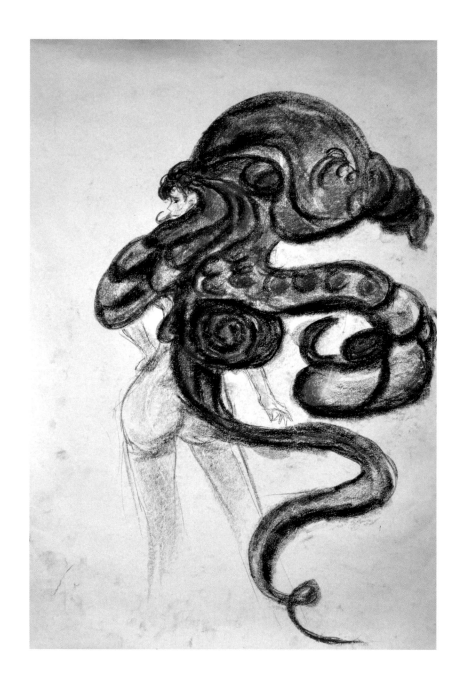

106

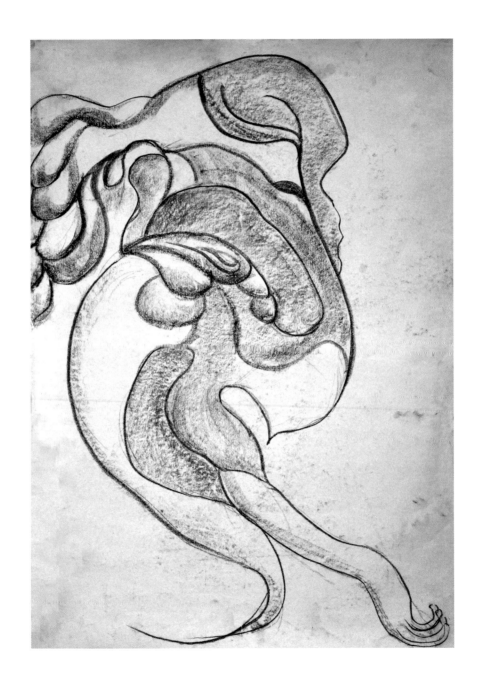

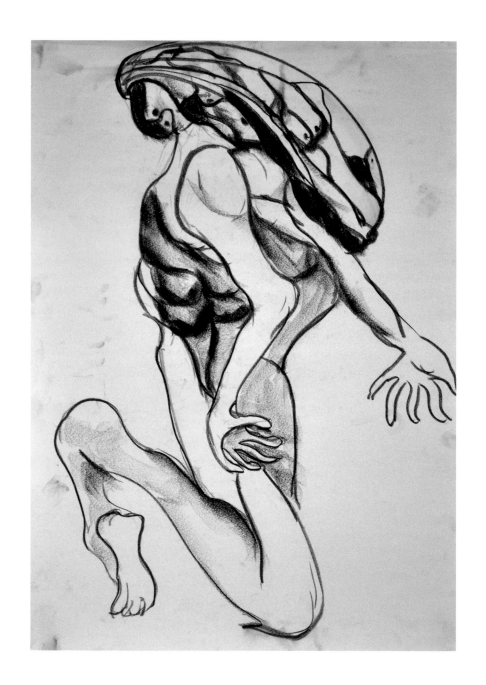

114

120

126

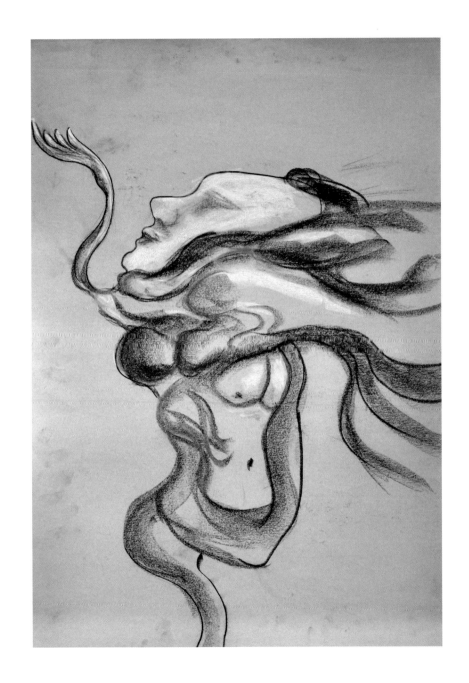

出版者 / 周士軒
圖文作者 / 周士軒
電話 / +886-2-27658315
地址 / 台北市松山區民生東路 5 段 184 號 14 樓之 2
E-mail / chou.hsuan@gmail.com
封面設計 / 周子荇
美術設計 / 陳彥鄍
印刷 / 飛燕印刷有限公司
　　　 23557 新北市中和區橋安街 17 號 6 樓
　　　 電話：+886-2-22476705
出版日期 / 2020 年 6 月
版次 / 初版
定價 / 新臺幣 480 元
ISBN / 978-957-43-7726-8（平裝）

Publisher / Sean Chou
Author / Sean Chou
Tel / +886-2-27658315
Address / 14F-2, No.184, Section 5, Ming Seng East
　　　　　Road, Song Shan District, Taipei, Taiwan.
E-mail / chou.hsuan@gmail.com
Cover Design / Jessy Chou
Designer / Chen Yan-chun
Printing / Feiyen Printing Co., Ltd.
　　　　　6F., No. 17, Qiao-an St., Chongho District,
　　　　　New Taipei City 23557, Taiwan.
　　　　　Tel：+886-2-22476705
Publish Date / June 2020
Edition / First Edition
Price / NTD 480
ISBN / 978-957-43-7726-8 (paperback)

ISBN 978-957-43-7726-8
9 789574 377268

故事崇拜

story
worship

周 士 軒
Sean Chou